W. Garrett (William Garrett) Horder

The supreme argument for Christianity: an appeal to facts

W. Garrett (William Garrett) Horder

The supreme argument for Christianity: an appeal to facts

ISBN/EAN: 9783741176319

Manufactured in Europe, USA, Canada, Australia, Japa

Cover: Foto ©Andreas Hilbeck / pixelio.de

Manufactured and distributed by brebook publishing software
(www.brebook.com)

W. Garrett (William Garrett) Horder

The supreme argument for Christianity: an appeal to facts

SMALL BOOKS ON GREAT SUBJECTS.

Pott 8vo, in Buckram Cloth, price 1s. 6d. each.

Small Books on Great Subjects.—XV.

THE SUPREME ARGUMENT FOR CHRISTIANITY.

By W. GARRETT HORDER.

First Edition, September, 1899.

THE SUPREME ARGUMENT FOR CHRISTIANITY.

An Appeal to Facts.

By W. Garrett Horder.

"If asked where, among all the Christian Churches of the age, the Gospel was to be found, he would answer, 'Where it has always been found, in the Christian life.'"

BENJAMIN JOWETT.

LONDON: JAMES CLARKE & CO.
13 & 14, Fleet Street.   1899.

"We may find in Christianity itself the principle that may revive Christianity."

SIR JOHN SEELEY.

Preface.

I HAVE long been impressed with the fact that large numbers of Christian people are craving for a simple proof of the Faith so precious to themselves—a proof which does not need, as the older ones did, a previous process of verification. It is useless, or almost so, nowadays, to point to prophecy or the miracles as authenticating Christianity, since both of these have first to be established before they can become valid arguments. Something simpler, something which all can verify for themselves, is now needed as a basis for faith.

Our Lord recognised this Himself when, in an age perplexed as to his claims, He pointed to a method of proof within the reach of all. "If any man willeth to do His will he shall know of the teaching, whether it be of God, or whether I speak of Myself." We cannot, therefore, be wrong in moving along a line thus opened by the great Founder of our Faith.

It is significant of this craving for a verifiable proof of Christianity, that the theologies which hold the field in Germany make their appeal chiefly to the facts of the Church's history, and the witness of the Christian experience. These are the dominant notes in the teachings of Albrecht Ritschl, and Willibald Herrmann, and, indeed, give the chief value to their writings. Certainly, they are an indication of the craving of the age for something which can be verified as a proof of Christianity.

Out of this conviction the lectures which follow grew.

It must not be concluded that, because I confine myself to this line of proof, I regard it as the only one; but it does seem the one likely to be of most service to the temper of the present time.

When these lectures had been delivered, I found that my conviction was well grounded, since from very different types of hearers—the learned and the unlearned, the critical and the believing—testimony reached me that help had been found in the argument here presented.

Although these lectures were fully reported in the local press, many and pressing requests for publication in a more permanent form reached me. To such requests I could not refuse compliance. I have, therefore, carefully revised and enlarged the lectures, and added references which may direct readers to fuller sources of information on this momentous subject.

I have thought it better to leave the lectures in the direct form in which they were first presented, believing that thus they would more fully effect their purpose with the larger company to which they are now addressed.

If, in any small measure, they tend to strengthen faith in those who already believe, or to quicken faith in those who now find it hard to believe, or to aid those who have to meet the opposition of the sceptical, I shall be deeply thankful.

Contents.

〰〰〰〰〰

The Change Wrought in the Apostles.

" The ideals of untramelled love for what is good, and of inward peace over against the world, which beam down as the sunshine upon the life of the Christian brotherhood, do not actually cause our faith in God, but they do lift us into an inward condition where the figure of Jesus, as history records it, touches us with such power that we are obliged to place confidence in it as a revelation of God."

WILLIBALD HERRMANN.

THE CHANGE WROUGHT IN THE APOSTLES.

"Now when they beheld the boldness of Peter and John, and had perceived that they were unlearned and ignorant men, they marvelled, and they took knowledge of them that they had been with Jesus."—ACTS IV. 13.

MANY kinds of proof have been presented on behalf of Christianity. A great literature has been put forth which used to be called "Evidences of Christianity," but which now goes under the name of "Apologetics." I do not like the name, since it seems to imply that we have to apologise for our Faith.

Every age has rested on evidences of its own. In earlier days those chiefly relied on were prophecy and miracles. We were pointed to the Old Testament, where the coming of the Messiah was foretold, and to the New Testament to see how those prophecies were fulfilled. We were pointed to the miracles, which were regarded as Divine attestations of the Christ. These for the time served their purpose, and supported the faith of men. But one great disadvantage of these methods of proof lay in this, that a previous process had to be gone through to establish the validity of the prophecies and of the miracles.

But then beyond this, as Tennyson says, "The thoughts of men are widen'd with the process of the suns," or, as Lowell says, "Time makes ancient good uncouth." And so, what served to support the faith of our fathers does not serve to support ours.

A new spirit is abroad. We look at the same Christ, but we look at Him with different eyes. We believe on the same Christ, but we believe on Him for different reasons. A book like Paley's "Evidences of Christianity" met the need of the age for which it was written, but it does not meet our needs, and so it has become in the main obsolete.

Every age needs evidences of its own, just as each age has its own methods of locomotion and communication. Our fathers travelled by stage coach and communicated by slow and costly posts; we travel by steam and communicate by telephone and telegraph. And as our outward ways alter, so do our inner thoughts. We cannot look at things through the eyes of our forefathers—it is not well that we should—we must look at them with our own eyes. Then we see better; see to more purpose. I do not say that the old evidences of Christianity are without value, but I do say that they are not of the same value to us as they were to the men of earlier ages. Bishop Butler did a great service by his book, "The Analogy of Religion," so did Archdeacon Paley by his book, "The Evidences of Christianity," because they met the difficulties of those ages; but they scarcely touch the needs of our time. And, therefore, I shall rather present ideas which have been aids to my own faith, and which I trust may prove to be so to yours.

There is a verse which has been called the Reviewer's canon, which runs thus:

In every work regard the author's end
Since none can compass more than they
    intend.

That verse used to be printed in a certain magazine over the review of books. Every book ought to be looked at in that light. And that principle applies to our Christian faith. We can only judge of Christianity in the light of its purpose. We have first of all to ask, What did

Christ come into the world to
do? When we have answered
that question — when we know
what He came to do—we can say
whether He has done it or not.
There is very little difficulty in
answering the question, — What
did Christ come to do? because
He Himself distinctly tells us,—"I
am come that they might have
life, and that they might have it
more abundantly." He puts the
same thing in a different form
when He says, "God so loved the
world that He gave His only be-
gotten Son, that whosoever be-
lieveth on Him should not perish,
but have eternal life." Life is
the keynote of both these great
utterances. And the life is not
the mere life of the body; men
had that before. It is not even
the mere life of the intellect; men
had that before; but "life which is
life indeed"—the life of the spirit.
Now, I want you to fix that
firmly and clearly in your mind—

that Jesus Christ came to give life;
life which from its intensity, not
simply because of its duration, He
called eternal life. He came to be
the open way through which the
life of God should flow into the
souls of men. He came to kindle
a divine life—the germ of which
was in men, breathed into them
by the breath of God. He came
to kindle that dormant germ into
active life. In the Gospels we see
Him engaged in this great work—
by His presence among men, by
His words, His deeds, His spirit,
His sacrifice, His victory over
death.   All these have one object
—to kindle life in men.

I do not stay to show that this
was the supreme need of men.
We all know that to be the case.
Tennyson expressed a world-wide
feeling when he wrote :

'Tis life, whereof our nerves are scant,
Oh life, not death, for which we pant ;
More life, and fuller, that I want.

Prometheus was called by the

Greeks the fire-bringer, but Christ was the life bringer.

And the supreme question is, did He accomplish this great purpose? Happily, this is a question we are in a position to answer. The answer is to be found in the first apostles, in Christendom, and in the Christian life. Of the first of these I now speak.

The Gospels show the Christ at work; the other books of the New Testament present the results of His work. In the Gospels we see the apostles being wrought upon by the great life-bringer. In the Acts of the Apostles and the Epistles we see the results of His work in their characters and lives. The Gospels may be compared to a workshop in which Christ is at work, not with His hands, but with His spirit—by word, by fellowship, by example, by sacrifice—infusing Himself into His apostles. In the after books we can judge whether He was success-

ful or not. The same men appear
in both—in the Gospels wrought
upon by Christ, and in the Acts
and Epistles revealing all unconsciously the results of His work.
I say all unconsciously, for they do
not pose as proofs or examples of
Christ's work—with an utter un-
consciousness of their uniqueness,
they express themselves. They
had no idea of being used as
evidences of Christianity; they
had no thought that their words
would be handed down the ages;
they spoke, they wrote in an art-
less, childlike way what they be-
lieved—they simply unveiled what
was in their hearts. Christ came
to give men life. These were the
first men with whom He came into
contact. Did He succeed? That
is the great question, a question
which the Acts and the Epistles
enable us to answer. If Christ
failed with these men, He would
probably fail with all men. If He
succeeded with these men, why

should He not succeed with all men?

Now, I say without hesitation that He succeeded, and for proof I point you to the self-revelations of these men in the New Testament. Nay, more, I say that He succeeded in every part of their nature. Life is a very pervasive thing. You can't shut life within any little enclosure of the being. Kindle a man's heart into vigorous life, and the life will run through every fibre of his being; it will touch every nerve and muscle and artery. He will step more firmly; he will grasp more tightly; he will look more animated. And quicken a man's spiritual life, and not spirit only but mind will be kindled. And it was thus with these apostles. This new life which Christ brought touched every part of their complex being.

First of all, consider the mental quickening it brought. To see this it is needful to remember that these men were not gathered out of the intellectual élite of the nation; they came from the un-lettered and ignorant class—from the company of fishermen or from the receipt of custom. Sometimes, it is true, among such classes bright spirits are found. John Bunyan is an illustration of this; but these men were not rough diamonds, they were dull, carnal, without spiritual insight. The gospels are full of proofs of this. Their stupidity tried Christ's patience to the uttermost. He cried, "How is it that ye do not understand?" "O fools and slow of heart." Never had teacher a duller class. Their only qualification for being there was that they felt the spell of Christ so as to follow Him. But they were dull of nature, and with no educa-tion to sharpen them. They had sat at the feet of no Rabbi; they did not even know the law.

But now look at them, when they had passed through Christ's

school. Look at them as they
stand revealed in the Acts of the
Apostles. What a change has
passed over them! Even mentally
they can hold, and more than
hold, their own with the Rabbis.
Their dulness, their unspirituality,
their clinging to the letter, these
have all gone. Life has touched
them, and even their minds have
been kindled. The ancient word
has in them been fulfilled—" The
entrance of Thy words giveth life;
it giveth understanding to the
simple." So great is the change
that we ask, Are these the same
men who put such stupid questions
to their Master?

We may ask, How could the touching of the heart quicken the mind?
It would be hard to believe that it
could, had we not seen, as we have,
stupid men under the influence of
religion grow wise and thoughtful.
The touching of the heart often
opens the eyes of the mind.

Look at these men in the school

of Christ in the Gospels; gather up all their silly questionings, and so form an estimate of their mental state, and then go on to the Acts of the Apostles, and you will see how the life-giver by touching their spirits has cleared and strengthened their minds.

I have not brought St. Paul into this account, because he *did* belong to a lettered company, and the change in him was of a somewhat different kind, but though it was different, it was equally striking. His mind was an educated one: but, mark you, it was educated in Rabbinical methods, and anything more formal, childish, silly, it is impossible to imagine. I wish you would read parts of the Talmud—the great book of the Jewish Rabbis*—and

* The Talmud belongs to a somewhat later age than that of St. Paul, but it represents the spirit and method of the Rabbinical schools of his age. It contains fine passages, but in the main it is utterly childish.

then pass from that to the Epistles of St. Paul, and you would see how great a change had come over this man, educated though he was.

I will give you a sample of the kind of subjects they discussed in the schools of the Rabbis. Tradition records that the ladder (mentioned Genesis xxviii. 12) was 8,000 miles wide. How was this arrived at? Thus: It is written, "And behold the angels of God ascending and descending upon it." Angels ascending being in the plural, cannot be fewer than two at a time, so that when they passed they were four abreast at least. In Daniel x. 6, it is said of the angel, "His body was like Tarshish," and there is a story that Tarshish extended 2,000 miles. So that for two ascending angels to pass two descending ones the ladder must have been 8,000 miles wide.

Paul, however, did not belong to

the class Christ taught; he did
not know Him after the flesh.   In
quite another way he was touched
by the life-giver, but the change
was equally great—in some senses
greater—for it is harder to change
the educated than the uneducated
—harder to root out foolish ideas
from the trained mind than to put
right ideas into the simple mind.
To turn the pedantic Rabbi Saul
into the spiritual Paul was perhaps harder than to turn untrained
fishermen into spiritual apostles.

Of course, the great realm in
which Christ has moved has been
the heart; but how wonderful the
changes of mind He has wrought.
How much richer the world is in
intellect through the work of Him
who cried, "I am come that they
might have life, and that they
might have it more abundantly."

*And now let us turn to another
and deeper realm—the heart.*   The
coming of life opened the eyes,
but it also softened the hearts of

these apostles. These men, like their age, were naturally hard. The hardness of their age is revealed in the Gospels—most clearly revealed in the Rabbis' treatment of Jesus. Our hearts grow indignant at the purposeless cruelties which mark the course of the rulers, as they hurried Jesus to the cross. And the apostles belonged to their age, and were touched by its spirit; they ever leant to the sterner side. Their devotion to their Master, which was good, prompted them to courses that were vindictive. Upon the Samaritans, who would not welcome Him, they would have called down fire from heaven. From His foes they would have protected Him by the unsheathing of the sword. The Jewish, like the Pagan, world was hard. And these first apostles were not exempt from the spirit of the age. Their hardness of heart was as difficult to treat as their dulness of mind.

But, difficult as the task was, it was accomplished by the great life-bringer.

How changed is the spirit which pervades these men as we see them in the Acts and in the Epistles! What gentleness of spirit breathes through their words! Those words are so familiar to us that we do not discern the marvellousness of the change. We do not realise the sternness of the spirit that pervaded their age, and so we do not realise what a revelation it was to the world to hear these gentle notes. Read the writings of even the best of that age, either of the Jewish or the Pagan world, and then pass to the letters of these apostles, and you will realise how vast the work Christ had accomplished in their hearts.

Think of Peter—he of the drawn sword—uttering words like this: "And account the long-suffering of our Lord is salvation." Think

of Saul, who made havoc in the
Church, and haled men bound to
prison, taking farewell of his
friends at Ephesus in those words
recorded in the twentieth chapter
of the Acts of the Apostles—
perhaps the loveliest words of farewell the world possesses —" And
now, behold, I go bound in the
spirit unto Jerusalem, not knowing
the things that shall befall me
there: save that the Holy Ghost
witnesseth in every city, saying
that bonds and afflictions abide
me. But none of these things
move me, neither count I my life
dear unto myself, so that I might
finish my course with joy, and the
ministry, which I have received of
the Lord Jesus, to testify the
gospel of the grace of God. And
now, behold, I know that ye all,
among whom I have gone preaching the kingdom of God, shall see
my face no more. Wherefore I
take you to record this day, that I
am pure from the blood of all

men.   For I have not shunned to
declare unto you all the counsel of
God.   Take heed therefore unto
yourselves, and to all the flock,
over the which the Holy Ghost
hath made you overseers, to feed
the Church of God, which He hath
purchased with His own blood.
For I know this, that after my
departing shall grievous wolves
enter in among you, not sparing
the flock.   Also of your own
selves shall men arise, speaking
perverse things, to draw away
disciples after them.   Therefore
watch, and remember, that by the
space of three years I ceased not
to warn every one night and day
with tears.   And now, brethren, I
commend you to God, and to the
word of His grace, which is able
to build you up, and to give you
an inheritance among all them
which are sanctified.   I   have
coveted no man's silver, or gold, or
apparel.   Yea, ye yourselves know
that these hands have ministered

unto my necessities, and to them
that were with me. I have shewed
you all things, how that so
labouring ye ought to support
the weak, and to remember the
words of the Lord Jesus, how
He said, It is more blessed to
give than to receive." (Acts xx.
22 to 35.) How astonished that
ancient world must have been
to hear such words as these! Or
take the gentle terms so distinctive
of the apostolic writings—love,
joy, peace, long-suffering, patience,
meekness, gentleness—words right
out of the heart—words of men
not sitting at ease amid pleasant
places, but treated as the offscour-
ing of the earth—everywhere
spoken against, everywhere perse-
cuted.* These men had peace.

---

* " Christianity places the milder virtues
in the forefront, quite as emphatically as
philosophy did the political ones. These
latter, however, are sufficiently enforced in
the practice of the great teachers whose
conduct exhibits heroism of the highest

Christ's promise was fulfilled : " In
the world ye shall have tribulation,
but in Me ye shall have peace."
These men had joy ; the joy of the
Lord was their strength. Their
outer course was one long way of
struggle and persecution. Out-
wardly, everything was against
them, but in their hearts the peace,
and even the joy, of the Lord. I
believe they were the happiest men
of their age. Christ promised them
not outward prosperity, or posses-
sion, or renown, but He did promise them peace. Did He fulfil His

type. Still, it is an undoubted fact that
Christianity has reversed the order of their
importance. Which, then, are right, the
writers of the New Testament or the
philosophers? The answer of these modern
times is, that the former were right and the
latter wrong. There can be no doubt that,
if during the last four thousand years the
milder virtues had occupied the place which
the heroic ones have held in the public
estimation, the happiness of mankind
would have been increased a thousand-
fold." [A Manual of Christian Evidence,
by Rev. C. A. Row, D.D., p. 100.]

promise? Their own writings show that He did.

He came with this word on His lips—"I am come that they might have life, and that they might have it more abundantly." Here are the men self-revealed, with this life possessing their natures—a life so rich and full that the language of that time is stretched to bursting point to express it, and which finds new forms in peace, joy, hope, love. Strange sounds were these to that hard world, but they have become familiar to us through the Apostles' writings, and still more through their Master's influence.

I contend, therefore, that Christ has done what He undertook to do. In that first age, with everything to oppose, He fulfilled His promise. Therefore, He is to be trusted. All the promises of God in Him are Yea. He is the Truth, as well as the Way and the Life.

And what He did in these first followers He will do in us, if we will only let Him. For let it be remembered it was not till their Master had been taken from their midst that these great results appeared. The spiritual did not grow till the visible Christ had passed from their sight. They did not know Him after the spirit till they had ceased to know Him after the flesh. In a very deep sense it was the unseen Christ who thus quickened new life in their hearts, and so our position is not very different from theirs. We, like them, have to do with the Christ in the unseen realm. And, if we will only let Him, He will do in us what He did in them, and our hearts will know, as did theirs, a peace which passeth all understanding—a joy that is unspeakable and full of glory.

The Change Wrought in Christendom.

"We receive, from every side about us, evidences of Christian faith and Christian love, and so we are pointed to Christ, and prepared to understand His Person. Thus, in spite of all the darkness which sin causes amid our human intercourse, we gain a vision of spiritual riches, which reveals to the maturest mind and to the heart of a child alike what is the perfect life of the spirit."

WILLIBALD HERRMANN.

THE CHANGE WROUGHT IN CHRISTENDOM.

"These that have turned the world upside down are come hither also."—ACTS XVII. 6.

IN the last chapter I pointed you to the apostles, as they stand self-revealed in the Acts and the Epistles, as an argument for Christianity. I endeavoured to show that Jesus Christ came to give men life—life more abundantly—and that, in those who first gathered around Him, such life was quickened; their minds and hearts alike were lifted into a new region. Every candid thinker must admit that, at all events in his first scholars, Christ accomplished the mission for which He came to earth.

But, now, I will move out into a wider region. Now I will point

you to Christendom as a proof, on
a much larger scale, of the power
and, therefore, of the truth of our
Christian faith.

Some will be surprised that I
should find in Christendom an
argument for our faith. Christendom seems an argument against,
rather than for, Christianity. The
New Testament seems to you full
of evidence of the life-giving
power of Christ; but, when you
pass beyond its history to that of
later times, that life-giving power
seems to wane. Christendom
seems to you a difficulty to be ex-
plained, rather than a proof of the
vitality of the Christian religion.

You look out upon the nations
which bear the Christian name,
and which collectively pass under
the name of Christendom, and
you see little evidence of the life-
giving power of Jesus Christ.
You are impressed rather with the
absence of such power. The
Christian nations are standing

ın deadly opposition to each other
—ranged in armed camps ready
to rend each other—the greater
part of their revenue spent upon
destructive, rather than construc-
tive, forces. One of the chief and
most honoured callings in these
nations is that of the soldier.
You see that the one great fear,
which hangs like a nightmare
over these nations, is that war
may break out, and all their
destructive forces be called into
action; that a European conflict
may arise, which would be a
veritable Armageddon—a death-
struggle for supremacy. And
you ask, Can such a Christendom
be called an argument for Christianity?

Then you look at the internal
condition of these so-called Christian nations, and you see the rich
growing ever richer, and the poorest ever poorer. You see an ever-
increasing luxury in the upper
classes and an ever - increasing

poverty in the lowest classes—the
upper classes adding acre to acre,
turning cultivated land on which
many earned a living into deer
forests, where men and women
have had to make way for beasts,
that hunters may have sport.
You see the dwellings of the
rich growing more palatial and
extended, and those of the poorest
ever more narrow and wretched,
so that there is scarcely room
to stretch their limbs or air
to breathe. You see one class,
with more than they can eat, so
that the very plentitude weakens
their appetite, and another class,
not knowing whence the next meal
may come, ever within sight of
starvation. You see one class
pampered in childhood and youth
with every luxury, and another
class driven to school by Act of
Parliament, which has decreed that
their minds shall be filled, whilst,
at the same time, their stomachs
may be empty.

You see in high and low alike
"the lust of the flesh, and the lust
of the eye, and the pride of life";
and then you ask, Is a Christendom
like this any proof of the life-
giving power of Jesus Christ?

Now you will see that I have
not attempted to minimise the
evils of Christendom. I have not
followed the Pharisee who thanked
God that he was not as other men.
I think I am as fully alive to
current evils as you can be. And
yet, with all these full in view, I
do see in Christendom an argument for Christ and Christianity,
and I hope, before I have finished,
you will too.

Now let it be remembered, first
of all, that the evils of Christendom, of which I have spoken, are
familiar to us all. They are near
and visible, whilst the still greater
evils of the world before Christ
came are unfamiliar—are too far
off to be visible. We are always
more impressed by the near than

the distant.   An accident in our own street distresses us more than an earthquake gulfing hundreds in sudden overthrow away in South America.   And so, the present evils of Christendom seem more to us than the far greater ones of the age before Christ.

When the Social Purity Crusade was at its height, I was present at a meeting in the north of London, where a lady, in an impassioned speech, declared that London was more impure than any of the cities of the ancient classical world.   It fell to my lot to speak after her, and I pointed out that, bad as London was in this respect, it was not nearly so bad as Pompeii or Rome in the olden time ; for London is ashamed of its impurity —it hides it away, covers it over— but these ancient cities felt no such shame.   They flaunted it in the face of day.   In London, the churches are against impurity ; but, in these cities of the olden time,

some of the most shameless haunts
of impurity were within the
temples, and some of the worst
offenders were the priests and
vestal virgins who represented religion.

Before we could judge of Christ's
work on the apostles, it was necessary to see what was their condition when they came under His
influence, and, to judge whether
Christ has made the world better,
we must know its state before He
came to give it life. Few people
know this, and so they do not see
the greatness of the work accomplished by Him. And what is
more, it is impossible in public to
make people know. As St. Paul
says, "It is a shame even to speak
of those things that are done by
them in secret." But, even within
the pages of the New Testament,
there are hints of the then condition of the world. Such hints are
to be found in the first chapter of
the Epistle to the Romans, whilst

3

in the first Epistle to the Corinth-
ians there is an indirect, but awful,
indication of the state of things in
the city of Corinth. Read those
chapters, and you will see how
practices most revolting clung even
to those who had come into the
Christian Church—those selected
and trained; and if such things
were done by them, what must
have been the state of the people
at large?

Mr. Matthew Arnold, a great
lover of the classical world, has
compressed into four memorable
lines the moral, or rather immoral,
condition of that world—

On that hard Pagan world disgust
And secret loathing fell.
Deep weariness and sated lust
Made human life a hell.

In those lines stress is laid on two
things—the hardness and impurity
of the ancient world. I will give
you a few illustrations of these
two things.

First, of its hardness. You are

all familiar, either through description or pictures, with the Colosseum at Rome—that vast building which dwarfs even the greatest of our modern ones, and which provided space for 80,000 spectators. Great as the Colosseum was, it was diminutive compared with the Great Circus, which, in Pliny's time, provided 260,000 seats, and afterwards was made to contain nearly half a million spectators. These great structures were the scenes of doings more bloody and cruel than any others of the western world. I would that the scenes there witnessed could be unrolled, as in a panorama, before your eyes. No other argument would be needed to show the vast change wrought in Europe by the Gospel of Jesus Christ. Let me indicate the kind of spectacle witnessed by the vast crowds of Rome in these places. "At the triumph of Aurelian 800 pairs of gladiators fought; during the games of Trajan 10,000. Sometimes female gladiators fought, sometimes dwarfs. The condemned were sometimes burnt in shirts of pitch to illuminate the gardens, or were hung upon crosses, and left to be torn by famished bears before the populace. Criminals, dressed in the skins of wild beasts were exposed to tortured and maddened bulls. Under Nero, 400 tigers fought with elephants and bulls. When the Colosseum was dedicated by Titus, 5,000 animals were killed. Platforms were constructed to drop in pieces at a signal, and launch those upon them into cages of devouring wild beasts; and, most horrible of all, naked women were bound by their hair to the horns of wild bulls that the lust and cruelty of the savage spectators might be gratified together.*

* Dr. S. R. Storr's " The Divine Origin of Christianity."

And, mark you, these doings were not confined to the capital city of Rome. They were imitated on a smaller scale all over the empire. You all know that remains of amphitheatres are still to be seen in many of the towns of France and Italy. Nearly one hundred and twenty of these have been discovered. In them scenes similar to those of the Roman Colosseum were witnessed—witnessed by all classes of the people.

You will say, Did not the priests or the philosophers or the moralists protest against such scenes? On the contrary, they were present as spectators; nay, more, these scenes were invested with a religious significance. On this point you shall have the testimony of Dr. Döllinger —one of the greatest, if not the very greatest scholar of recent days :—" The sacerdotal colleges and authorities," says Arnobius, " flamens, and augurs, and chaste vestals, all have seats at these

public amusements. There are
seated the collective people and
senate, consuls and consulars,
while Venus, the mother of the
Roman race, is danced to the life,
and in shameless mimicry is represented as revelling through all the
phases of meretricious lust. The
great mother, too, is danced; the
Dindymene of Pessinus, in spite of
her age, surrendering herself to
disgusting passion in the embraces
of a cowherd. The supreme ruler
of the world is himself brought in,
without respect to his name or
majesty, to play the part of an
adulterer, masking himself in
order to deceive chaste wives, and
take the place of their husbands
in the nuptial bed. He then
describes how the whole assembly
rises, and makes the vast space of
the theatre echo with a tumult of
applause, when the gods themselves are bespattered with all the
ridicule and contempt of these
comedies; and thus, says Augus-

tine, the very gods were laughed to scorn in the theatres who were worshipped in the temples." *

The hardness of the ancient world was shown not merely in the public spectacles, but in individual action. That hardness was awfully manifested in relation to children, who, when they happened to be female, or were not wanted, were exposed, so that cold, or hunger, or cruel beast or bird, might put an end to their existence. Quintilian said that "to kill a man is often held to be a crime; but to kill one's own children is sometimes considered a beautiful action among the Romans." "The infants thus abandoned were gathered sometimes by witches, to use their bodies in incantations, or more frequently by slave-dealers to train as female slaves or prostitutes." The favourite places for such exposure in Rome were near the

* The Gentile and the Jew in the Courts of the Temple of Christ. Vol. II. p. 195.

Lactarian column and in the Velabrum, a district near Mount Aventine. To these places those who desired children for adoption, or for nefarious purposes, were in the habit of resorting.*

Some of the Roman emperors—Severus and Diocletian—did their best to stop these practices: the Stoics pleaded and wrote against them, but in vain. It was not till the dynamic of Christian feeling arose, that provision was made by hospitals for the reception of foundlings, and afterwards, by the quickened sense of the value of human life, that the cruel practice of exposure was brought to an end.

Indeed, it was not till Christianity arose that the glory and beauty of childhood became evident to the eyes and hearts of men. It is said that, in all classical literature, no passage can be found which discerns and sets forth the glory and beauty of the child-life. Our eyes

* Gesta Christi, p. 75.

have been opened to these by the new feeling quickened by Him Whose eyes rested on children with a deeper delight than on those of riper age, and Who saw in them the chief characteristics of citizenship in the Kingdom of God.

Another illustration of the hardness of pagan life is to be found in slavery, which existed on a larger scale, and in more terrible forms, in the classic than the modern world. As to the extent of slavery, some indications are found in such facts as these: "A law of Augustus forbade a poor exile from carrying away with him more than twenty slaves; another reduced the number which could be maintained by testamentary provisions, making one hundred the maximum, which, from the proportions mentioned, would indicate that five hundred was not an uncommon number to be owned by one person. We hear, from Seneca, of a master counting the roll of his slaves as a general

counts his soldiers. Tacitus speaks
of the city becoming frightened at
the increasing number of slaves.
A proposition was made in the
Senate to indicate the slaves by
their dress, but was dropped because of the danger that the slaves
would outnumber the freemen."*

Some idea may be gained of the
terrible forms slavery assumed from
such facts as these: "The story of
Pollio, a Stoic, is well known, as
related by Seneca; how he amused
himself by feeding his fish with
fragments of his mutilated slaves.
Many were furnished to the amphitheatres to be killed in public
festivals. Old and infirm slaves
were abandoned to die of hunger."†

Slavery has now practically come
to an end; but, when we say that
its end came through the influence
of the spirit of Christianity, we
are met by several objections—that
the Apostles tolerated slavery;

* Gesta Christi, p. 49.
† Ibid 47.

that St. Paul did not bid Philemon liberate Onesimus, but only to treat him as a brother beloved; that the Church carried on no propagandum against it; that slave-holders were admitted to the Church's fellowship; that, in later ages, sóme of the staunchest upholders of slavery bore the Christian name, notably in America. It must be frankly admitted that the Church, as a Church, did little or nothing to abolish slavery; that at certain periods of her history she defended the system. On the surface, therefore, it looks as if the cause of the slave owed little or nothing to Christianity. But then the Church is not always to be taken as a synonym for Christianity—in many a dark period she has rather been an antonym. Certainly the Church did not abolish slavery, but the spirit of Christianity did, and that spirit found expression, not through the Church, but through certain elect and holy souls, such as John Woolman, William Lloyd Garrison, John Greenleaf Whittier, Theodore Parker, in America; and through Thomas Clarkson, William Wilberforce, and Granville Sharp, in England. It was the Christian spirit in such men that nerved their arm to strike so nobly for the freedom of the slave. It is always difficult to trace the operations of spiritual feeling—far more difficult than to trace the working of organised bodies, but can any one doubt that, but for the Christian dynamic, slavery would still be one of the recognised institutions of the world? Christ, it is true, uttered no word against slavery; on that, as on a multitude of questions, He was silent, but He laid down great principles, and quickened a spirit which made for the overthrow of every evil, and the institution of a kingdom in which righteousness alone can reign.

It has been well said :

"The fetters did not fall from
the slave, but they became golden
fetters. Labour was ennobled, it
was lifted from the dust and set
upon a throne. The association
of toil with infamy was broken
for ever, and a new association
was formed in its room. The
rough work of the hands was re-
flected by that light which makes
all things beautiful. It was taken
up into Christian thought, amal-
gamated with Christian life, and
made an essential part of Christian practice, and, in the process
of elevation, all the disgrace dropt
from it, and left it transformed.
It was such a transformation as
we see in the idea of the Cross
itself; it had once been the badge
of the slave; it was now the
banner of the hero. The state of
servitude remained, but the act of
the servitude was exalted, and it
was inevitable that the exaltation
of active labour should ere long

reflect its lustre on the personal condition of the slave."*

With such a spirit as I have attempted to describe abroad in the Pagan world, is it any wonder that human life, when it ceased to be of value to the State, was reckoned unworthy of care? Is it any wonder that female children and old people were left to perish outside the city walls? Is it any wonder that no provision existed for the sick among the poor, or for the blind, the deaf, the crippled, the idiot, the insane?

Go over the ruined remains of the city of Pompeii, which, as you all know, was suddenly buried by a storm of ashes from Vesuvius, about the beginning of the Christian era, and so was almost hermetically sealed and preserved to our own time, and you will find temples, forums, theatres, baths, mansions, shops, but no relics of

* Dr. Matheson's "Growth of the Spirit of Christianity."   Vol I., p. 305.

anything like a hospital or asylum or refuge for the distressed; abundant signs of luxury, taste, commerce, religion, but no sign of philanthropy, pity, mercy. At Athens there was an altar to Pity, but it had no worshippers.

It has been well said that "neither the religion nor the philosophy of Rome tended to comfort the poor. The divinities were cruel; the Stoic affected to despise the sufferings of the indigent; the Epicurean took no thought of them. Throughout the vast region of Mogul, India, China, the use of hospitals is unknown to this day. In no country did Christianity find such institutions existing. The history of their rise and progress can be traced in few words. In the year 380 the first hospital in the West was founded by Fabiola, a devout Roman lady, within the walls of Rome. St. Jerome says expressly, 'This was the first of all.' And he adds that it was a

country-house destined to receive
the sick and the infirm, who,
before, used to be stretched on
the public ways."

Surely enough has been said to
prove that the Pagan world was
hard.

*Of the impurity of the ancient
world it is still harder to speak;*
indeed, it is impossible to speak of
it save by the slightest hints.   If
it were possible to tell of things to
be seen in Pompeii, or in the
Pompeian Museum at Naples, you
would want no other evidence of
the awful impurity of the time
preceding the Christian era.   Take
my word for it, they are too awful
to be even hinted at, much less
described.

There are two features of this
impurity which render it the more
awful, and must be named.

*The first is, that no shame was
felt about it.*   It was flaunted in
the eye of day.   Like drink in our
day, impurity had its sign-boards.

Things that now we dare scarcely
refer to, were unblamed, and
brought no dishonour. The lowest
hell is reached when sin wakens
no shame, or when, as then, men
gloried in their shame. Whilst
shame remains, there is hope;
when this departs, hope droops
her wings.

In the most powerful, if not the
most beautiful, sonnet she ever
wrote, Miss Rossetti says :—

Shame is a shadow cast by sin: yet
    shame
Itself may be a glory and a grace,
Refashioning the sin-disfashioned face;
A nobler bruit than hollow-sounded
    fame,
A new-lit lustre on a tarnished name,
One virtue pent within an evil place,
Strength for the fight, and swiftness for
    the race,
A stinging salve, a life-requickening
    flame.
A salve so searching we may scarcely live,
A flame so fierce it seems that we must
    die.
An actual cautery thrust into the heart :
Nevertheless, men die not of such smart;

And shame gives back what nothing
    else can give,
Man to himself,—then sets him up on
    high.

But, not only had shame departed, impurity had actually
acquired a religious sanction.
Minucius Felix indicates that, in
his time, the chambers of the
temple-keepers saw more licen-
tiousness than the brothels themselves. The very gods were ap-
pealed to as supreme examples
of licentious appetite, giving
authority to the like among
men.

It has been truly said that "No
frightfullest periods in licentious-
ness in Europe, in profligate courts,
or in loose and promiscuous seafar-
ing populations, have approached,
in utter and shameless sensuality,
the period of the Empire, when
the new religion, by apostle, evan-
gelist, and devoted disciple, began
to be preached in it."

Of the unnatural vices, which so

corrupted the Greek and Roman world, it is impossible to speak— the subject is abhorrent to our modern ears, but in classic times these were spoken of without a blush.* Of these Plato speaks with a despairing sadness, and regards their abolition as remote as in our day prostitution or the doing away of war is by the mass of the people. "Three principles or moral forces," he says in the "Laws," "may break up these evils : first, those of piety or love to a Divine person ; second, the desire for honour or the respect of the good ; and thirdly, the love of moral beauty—that not of the body but of the soul." † It will be noticed that all these forces were provided in Christianity, and through its influence the accursed

* It is significant that Juvenal, who in those times used to be read even to ladies, has now to be expurgated for modern use. Some of his passages are too coarse to be presented even in their original tongue.

† Gesta Christi.

thing has been overcome ; or, if not
quite overcome, has been set in so
keen a light, that its enormity has
been realised, and the sporadic
recrudescene of it has been
visited with the most condign
penalty of the law and the scorn
of all noble souls.

Another illustration of the
impurity of the Pagan world may
be found in the relation between
the sexes which then prevailed.
The marriage - tie was of the
slightest, and was broken under
the smallest pretexts. Seneca
speaks of daily divorces, and he
tells of illustrious and noble-born
women who reckon their years not
by the number of the consuls,
but by that of their husbands.
Juvenal has a well-known epigram
on the woman who had eight husbands in five years. Tertullian
represents divorce as the very purpose and end of Roman marriage.

Let all deductions be made
which should be made from such

representations—for doubtless even in that age there were those who lived purer lives—yet it is clear that the sanctity which, under Christianity, has grown up around marriage, was then very rare, if not quite unknown. This seems certain, that the religion of that time did little or nothing to hallow the marriage-tie.

Both in this country, and still more in America, marriage is too often treated as a matter of convenience, and dissolved without sufficient reason. But this is the case chiefly among those beyond the pale of Christianity. Whereever Christ's influence reaches, marriage is always regarded as the holiest union possible between the sons and daughters of men.

Very unwillingly have I spoken of these things; one would far rather be silent about them. But in a day like ours, in which men cry out for a Pagan Renaissance, it is needful to indicate what

Paganism produced. Those who
desire its return know not what
they seek.

Then, too, it is needful to have
some idea of what the world then
was, that we may see what we owe
to Jesus Christ. Earnest hearts
are often so oppressed with the
evils of Christendom to-day, that
they fancy Christ's work has been
in vain. They need to give heed
to Matthew Arnold's words—

Perceiv'st thou not the change of day?—
  Ah! Carry back thy ken,
What, some two thousand years! Survey
  The world as it was then!

Like ours it look'd in outward air.
  Its head was clear and true,
Sumptuous its clothing, rich its fare,
  No pause its action knew;

Stout was its arm, each thew and bone
  Seem'd puissant and alive—
But, ah! its heart, its heart was stone,
  And so it could not thrive!

Yes, its heart was stone, and so
it could not thrive. But Christ
has touched men's hearts; they

cannot but feel the evils that still remain, and out of that feeling will grow the energy by which they will be, at last, overcome. It was by a heart that had been touched with the love of Christ that the frightful cruelties of the Colosseum were brought to an end. Moved by that love, the young monk Telemachus leaped into the arena, gave his life, and so sealed the doom of those cruel games. It was by that same love moving in the hearts of men that slavery was gradually brought to an end in the Roman empire. That same love, quickening compassion for men, will yet grapple with, and, at last, overcome the great evils which still remain, and which so distress our hearts.

The world is still very far from being a kingdom of God, but it is immensely nearer than it was when Christ came into our midst. We date our years from the time of His advent. And what does

that mean? Surely this — that
then the world made a new
departure. It *was* a new departure. "The sun of righteousness
arose with healing in his wings."
Light came, and, with it, hope.
The light has not yet scattered
the darkness, but it is not to-day
the gross darkness of the first
years of our era.

Two things are quite certain.
We have ceased to glory in our
sin; we have become ashamed of
it. There is still plenty of sin;
but it does not stalk forth in the
light; it seeks the darkness. That
is a great step in advance. Shame
is the first step to better things.
And shame will deepen as the
light grows, until, at last, it will
make us put off the works of
darkness, and put on the armour
of light.

And, then, no longer does sin
find sanction in religion. Oh,
how awful is it when religion,
which should be a light, becomes

darkness, when it favours, rather than represses, sin. Christ has indeed cleansed our temples. They are not as yet what they should be, but the awful intruder impurity has been driven forth. And the churches of to-day, in spite of all their faults, are bent on co-working with Christ for the redemption of men. And every day the area of that redemption widens to their view. Once they thought only of the soul; now they think of the whole being—body, soul, and spirit. Once they worked only on Sundays; now their activities run all through the week. Here are grounds of confidence.

Through these nineteen centuries we have been turning from the darkness, and moving toward the light. Often the advance has been slow; often there has been a halt; often the life has grown weak, but, again and again, the Christian company has been touched with new life and has pressed on, till we

are nearer the light to-day than
ever we were before.

Look at the years before Christ,
and the years after, and you will
see that, before He came, men were
hopeless ; since, they have been
hopeful. When hope dies, advance
is impossible. When hope arises,
advance is certain.

Let me note two things, before
I close.

First, Christ has not yet redeemed the world ; but the only
hope of its final redemption is in
the nations which bear His name
and are touched, however slightly,
with His spirit. Blot these from
the world, and what hope for the
race remains ? God knows that
they have faults and sins enough ;
but, in spite of these, they are the
only hope for the world. Only in
them is life to be found. What
prospect would there be for the
race if these were blotted out ?
Can any ray of light be found in
the non-Christian lands, such as

India or China, civilised when we
were barbarians? They are to-day
where they were centuries ago.
Max Müller says that the India
of the villages to-day is the India
of three thousand years ago. No;
the future of the world is with the
Christian nations; presently the
world will be under their sway.
Yes, and chiefly under the sway
of those nations that cleave closest
to the simplicity of Christ. The
simpler the faith in Christ, the
greater the power of the nation.
In spite of all its faults, Christendom is a great witness for Christ.
In it, if the Nazarene has not yet
conquered, He is on the road to
conquest.

Second, people sometimes say, or
if they do not say they think, surely
nineteen centuries are enough for
Christ to have completed His
work and redeemed the world.
And so it would have been, if the
world had wanted to be redeemed.
But it did not; it resisted the

redemption. The apostles desired redemption, and so Christ accomplished His work in them — accomplished it in three short years. The delay of the world's redemption is due, not to want of power in Christ, but want of receptiveness in the world; for redemption is only possible through the co-operation of men. It cannot be accomplished by fiat or power. When the world craves redemption, Christ's work will be speedily accomplished. And what is true of the world is true of the individual. At closed doors Christ knocks in vain. He will not, cannot, force an entrance. Let the door be opened, and see if He will not accomplish His mighty work. Test Him for yourselves. Open your hearts for Him to work, and then you will need no other argument; you will have the witness in yourselves. Like the blind man of old, you will be able to say, "Whereas I was blind, now I see."

The Change as seen in the Christian Life and Experience.

"In its commencement and in all its development alike, Christian faith is nothing else than trust in persons and in the power of personal life. We begin to understand God's gift and God's help in our religious intercourse with Christians and through our reverence for them; then, when we have received such a training, the picture of that wonderful personal life which the Gospels set before us, becomes an earnest plea that we shall put our trust in it as testimony concerning a Man whose existence in our world makes us certain of God." WILLIBALD HERRMANN.

"The scientific life is less noble than the Christian; it is better, so to speak, to be a citizen in the New Jerusalem than in the New Athens; it is better, surely, to find everywhere a brother and friend, like the Christian, than like the philosopher, ' to disregard your relative and friend so completely as to be ignorant not only how he gets on, but almost whether he is a human being or some other creature.'" * SIR JOHN SEELEY.

* Plato, Theaet., p. 80.

THE CHANGE AS SEEN IN THE CHRISTIAN LIFE AND EXPERIENCE.

"Verily I say unto you, Among them that are born of women there hath not arisen a greater than John the Baptist; yet he that is but little in the kingdom of heaven is greater than he."—MATTHEW XI. 11.

THESE are very startling words— so startling that we ask, Can they be indeed true? For, remember, they put us, if we are really in the kingdom of heaven, in a higher place than the greatest of the Hebrew prophets. If we have any modesty in us, we shrink from claiming so high a position. We greater than John the Baptist! No, infinitely less, is our reply. And in one sense this is so. Have any of us the vigour, the courage, the self-sacrifice, which marked the great forerunner of the Christ?

But in another sense, if we are in the kingdom of heaven, we are greater than he—greater in privilege, greater in the spirit that works within us, greater in the vision of God before our eyes. This will be made more clear by an illustration. There is not one of us the equal in nature of, say, Socrates, the great philosopher of the olden time, and yet, in another sense, we are greater, since our minds are enriched with the wondrous things which science has discovered in the ages since he lived. A boy looks out on the world, and sees it more rightly than did the great Socrates. Our nature is not equal to his, but, since our lot has been cast in an age which has been so enlightened, we are, in the sense of privilege and knowledge, greater than he. And Christ did not mean that every citizen of the kingdom of heaven was greater in nature than John the Baptist, but that, being

in the kingdom of heaven, his
nature had been enriched with
thoughts and feelings which lifted
him to a higher position than the
great preacher of repentance.

And that is what I wish to set
forth before you—that the experience and life of a Christian are of
a richer and higher kind than
those of any outside that kingdom,
whether they lived before or since
Christ came. In that experience
and life lies the supreme proof of
our Christian faith.

As I have said in previous lectures, Jesus Christ came to give
men life—life more abundantly—
and if in those who yield to Him
such life is found, then His claim
is made good. The healed sufferer
is the best proof of the physician's
skill, and men whose life has been
quickened are the best proof of the
skill and power of Him who came
to give eternal life.

Now, the glory of this life which
Christ gives can only be rightly

seen when contrasted with that which men possessed before. Nothing is rightly seen save by contrast. If we had never known darkness, we should not realise the glory of light. If we had never been ill, we should not appreciate the value of health. And so we cannot realise the glory of the Christian experience and life, save on the dark background of men who did not possess these.

In previous lectures I tried to set forth the greatness of Christ's work in the apostles, by showing what they were before He wrought upon their natures. I tried to show the glory of Christendom by revealing the horrible pit and miry clay from which it had been brought. And the glory of the Christian experience and life can scarcely be realised, save by comparison with those who did not possess these. We are so familiar with these, since we have all our days been surrounded by Christian folk, that we do not see the full significance of the Christian life and character. We need, as Matthew Arnold said, to perceive the change of day—to carry back our ken some two thousand years, to the time before Christ touched the hearts of men.

It may be said, of course, that there are those around us to-day destitute of this Christian life and experience; and that is sadly true. But even those do not reveal to us what men are without Christ's influence, for even they have been touched, in some measure, by Jesus Christ. No dweller in a Christian land is untouched by Christianity, for it is, to some extent, in our laws, our manners, our social atmosphere. Even the opponents of Christianity are other than they would have been if Christ had not been made known in their land. To find the true contrast to the Christian life we must rather go back to the age before Christ, or to the lands where the Gospel has not as yet reached. Then the blindest must see how glorious is the work He has wrought in the hearts of men.

Let me try to indicate this— first, as to the origination of this life; second, in the life itself; and third, in the expressions of that life.

Firstly, as to the origination of this life. I mean by the origination of this life, conversion. Of the reality of what we call conversion, or, as it is called in the New Testament, turning — turning to God—there can be no dispute. That is a fact as certain as any fact of geology, or botany, or astronomy, and far more important, since what concerns the human spirit is of greater moment than what concerns only the material world. Conversion is a fact, and must be treated as such.

Of course, it is most *evidently* a fact when it is sudden, when there

is a great crisis in the life, when
the soul comes to a parting of the
ways, and turns from the broad to
the narrow way, from the path
which leads to destruction to that
which leads to life. Then it is
most evident. Then, not only is
the soul itself conscious of it, but
those around are conscious of it,
through the change of course.

But it is none the less real, none
the less a fact, when it is gradual,
when there is, little by little, a
shrinking from evil and a turning to good, when the earthly
grows less attractive and the
heavenly more attractive to the
soul. The fact, not the manner,
is the thing of importance.

In the great majority of cases
conversion is so gradual as to be
almost imperceptible, the journey
so slow that the certainty that it
has been travelled is known only
by arrival at the goal; but, in other
cases, where the soul had journeyed
into a far country, there is a

sharp and sudden resolution to return to the Father's home.

Conversion, however, is one of the facts which meets us in the Christian realm. There are lives whose whole direction has been turned, whose whole spirit has been altered. They meet us in every age; some of them stand out with great distinctiveness, because of the natures in which they took place, or the sudden way in which they were affected.

Now, I will not point you to what may be called the great classical examples of conversion, such as that of Augustine in the early Church, or of John Bunyan or John Newton in the later. I will give examples from our own day; I will take two narrated in the recently published life of Professor Drummond. I will give you the first in his own words. Speaking at one of the meetings for students he held in Edinburgh, he said: " There may be some here to-night who were here some years ago, when these meetings had their first beginning, and you may remember me reading a letter which was characterised by some of you as 'A letter from hell.' You remember, it was a frightful revelation of a tortured, sunken, lost human soul. It was anonymous, and signed 'Thanatos' — the Greek word for 'death.' Years have gone by, and I have not forgotten that man; and, if ever I thought a man was hopelessly, irretrievably lost, it was that man. He was an intellectual, physical, and moral wreck. I thought that case an impossibility. Gentlemen, I have in my pocket to-night a letter from 'Thanatos,' which he sent me this week, and he says he is, at last, a changed man, a new creature in Christ Jesus. He says the new life has choked the old, and that he is now in a position of responsibility and usefulness in this country."

I will quote another case, in some senses more extraordinary. Professor Drummond got a letter from an Edinburgh student, full of Agnosticism and even Atheism. He saw him, and could not make the slightest impression on him. Soon after, he saw this man in a meeting, and, by him, another whom he had occasionally seen there. The Professor went up to the latter to find out about this sceptic, and, to his amazement, learnt ˌthat the one he addressed was a graduate of an American University, who had come to Edinburgh to take a postgraduate course. In the dissecting-room he was placed next to the sceptic. He found him a man of remarkable ability, but without religion. He thought he might do something for him. He further said he was about to pack his trunks to go back to America, and then he thought of this friend, and wondered whether a year of his life would be better spent by going to start his profession in America or by staying in Edinburgh and trying to win that man for Christ. He said to himself, "My dear fellow, it will pay you to stay; you will get that man." Two or three months after, the last meeting of the students was held, at which they celebrated the communion, and Professor Drummond saw the sceptic sitting by this American, and handing the communion-cup to him. He had got his man, and a week after was on his way back to America.

That is a witness not only to the reality of conversion, but also to that altruistic element in the Christian character so rarely found in any other.

Now, I have an impression that such changes are peculiar to the Christian faith, or, if not absolutely peculiar, they are more distinctive of it than of any other faith of the world. I doubt very much whether anything like this

can be found in Mohammedanism,
or Confucianism, or Brahmanism,
or Buddhism.   In these, I fancy
—I do not speak with absolute
certainty—if there be conversion,
it is only the acceptance of the
particular   doctrines   of   these
religions.   I imagine that, if I
sought to be enrolled as a Mohammedan, all that would be required
would be the acknowledgment of
Mohammed as the Prophet of
Allah.   And so in relation to the
other faiths of the world.   But it
is not thus with our Christian
faith. Our Protestant missionaries
in many lands could easily fill
their churches, if they were willing
to receive all who just acknow-
ledge Jesus Christ, if they made
no demand for inward change,—
change of heart gradually expressing itself in change of life.

But, be this as it may, the
changes wrought in human character—wrought not merely on
the surface, but wrought deep

down in the nature, working from
the centre to the circumference—
and in all kinds of natures, not in
one class only, but in all classes,
the rich and the poor, the high
and the low, the learned and
ignorant, the credulous and the
critical—these form to my mind a
surpassing argument for our Christian faith, since they show that
what Christ came to do, He has
accomplished. The great cry, " I
am come that they might have life,
and that they might have it more
abundantly," has been ratified by
changes which have turned men
from darkness to light.

*Secondly, the Christian life in
itself.* That life is unique—unlike
anything the world ever saw before.
I do not mean that the world
never saw anything beautiful in
character before Christ came, or
apart from Him. I do not say, as
did one of the Fathers, that "the
virtues of the heathen were only
splendid vices." Virtue is virtue

wherever it be found, whether in heathendom or Christendom. For my part, I believe that virtue, wherever found, is prompted by the Light that lighteneth every man that cometh into the world. And to call good evil, because we cannot trace its connection with faith in Jesus Christ, is to come perilously near to what is described in Scripture as the sin against the Holy Ghost.

I daresay some of you know that, in the Westminster Confession of Faith, works done by the unregenerate, though they may be things God commands and of good use, are declared to be sinful. That is a fiction of the theologians, not a truth of Scripture. I should like to give you an illustration of how candid observation of life refutes that idea. The illustration comes from one who had accepted that doctrine. Dr. Ebenezer Brown started one day to preach at North Ferry, about two miles from his own town,

Inverkeithing. It was a wild,
drifting, dangerous day, but he
would go. The pony stumbled on
through the blinding snow, but all
the while the Doctor was thinking of
the sermon he was going to preach.
Half-way on his journey, the pony
staggered about, and at last upset
his master in the ditch by the
roadside. The feeble, helpless old
man might have perished there,
had not some carters, bringing up
whiskey casks from the Ferry, seen
the catastrophe, rushed up, raised
him to his feet, and, in their blunt
speech, exclaimed, " Puir auld
man, what brocht ye here sic a
day?" They put on his hat,
sorted, and cheered him. Then
one of these cordial ruffians
pierced a cask, and brought him
a horn of whiskey, saying, "Tak
that; it'll hearten ye." He took
the horn, and, bowing to them,
said, " Sirs, let us give thanks; "
and there by the roadside, with
the storm raging around, he asked

a blessing on it and for his kind
deliverers, before he took a taste
of the horn. The men cried like
children. They lifted him on his
beast, and one went with him to
Inverkeithing. To everybody they
met they repeated the story, and
broke down in tears when they
came to the blessing. "And to
think of asken' a blessing on a
tass of whiskey!" At the next
Presbytery, Dr. Brown rose and
said, "Moderator, I have something personal to say. I have
often said that real kindness
belongs only to real Christians,
but"—and then he told the story
of these men. "More true kindness I never experienced than
from these lads. They may have
had the grace of God, I don't
know; but I never mean again to
be so positive in speaking of this
matter."*

It is not needful, in order to

* "Horæ Subsecivæ" by Dr. John Brown.

appreciate Christianity, to depreciate the virtues found in humanity; but no one, who has considered the subject, can fail to see that Christianity has fashioned a type of character higher than the world ever knew before.

Take, if you will, the choicest specimens of which we have any knowledge—I mean such men as Epictetus and Marcus Aurelius, and I know not where to look, outside Christianity, for men who rose as high as they did; and I think you will feel that, great and noble as they were, they did not rise to the height of such men as St. Paul, or Augustine, or Bishop Wilson, or Fletcher of Madeley, or John Woolman. No! these men, as their name Stoic implies, had schooled themselves to endurance—to bear the ills that came to them, rather than seek to overcome them. They were content with the first part of St. Paul's precept, "Be not overcome of evil"; they

had not hope enough to strive to
overcome evil with good. In a
word, they were Stoics. That
word had once a noble sound,
because men were content to hold
their ground against evil, but
since Christ came, the word has
gained an ignoble signification;
it is no praise of a man nowadays
to say he is Stoical. The higher
ideal of Christ has made what
once seemed noble, to seem ignoble.

It was something, in a world
given over to despair, for men to
stand their ground against evil;
but, in a world touched with hope
by Jesus Christ, it is not enough
to endure. We must go on to
overcome evil, not merely in ourselves, but in others.

Then, beyond this, these Stoics
were content with personal
character — to take heed unto
themselves. They cared nothing,
they did nothing, to uplift the
men and women around. They
had little, if any, of that " enthu-

siasm of humanity," which is one of the characteristic features of the Christian faith.

Men read their writings, and they say, " What wonderful morality is here; there is little difference between it and that of Jesus Christ?" So really is this the case, that some have held that Seneca borrowed from, and even corresponded with, St. Paul. Yes, the morality is very high, but then a faith is not to be judged by precepts, but by the power it gives to embody those precepts in life. Matthew Arnold once described religion as "morality touched with emotion." These Stoics had the morality, but without the touch of emotion, by which it could be translated into life.

Ideals are not enough; there must be the dynamic to urge to their pursuit. Like Ovid, we are obliged to say, "I see the better, but take the worse, way." To see the better way is not enough;

there is needed the constraint, as St. Paul would say, to take it. Augustine discerned this, when he said that in Plato and Cicero he met with many utterances which were beautiful and wise, but, among them all, he never found, " Come unto me all ye that labour and are heavy laden, and I will refresh you." And from want of such a constraint—the constraint of love—these Stoics did not influence their fellows as did St. Paul, or as the humblest Christian does. They stood alone. Their goodness was not infectious; it did not reproduce itself in others. They looked on their own things, not on the things of others. Dean Farrar well says, " The very existence of such men is in itself a significant comment upon the Scriptural decision, that ' the world by wisdom knew not God.' For how many like them, out of all the records of antiquity, is it possible to count? Are there five

men, in the whole circle of ancient
history and literature, to whom we
could, without a sense of incon-
gruity, accord the title of 'holy'?
When we have mentioned Socrates,
Epictetus, and Marcus Aurelius, I
hardly know of another. Just men
there were in multitudes—men
capable of high actions; men
eminently worthy to be loved;
men, I doubt not, who, when the
children of the kingdom shall be
rejected, shall be gathered from
the East and the West with
Abraham, Isaac, and Jacob, into
the kingdom of heaven. Yes, just
men in multitudes; but how many
righteous, how many holy?"

There is a great difference between the just and the good.

But Christendom has been fruit-
ful in good men, in holy men,
not merely in high places, but
in lowly ones, not merely
among the learned, but among
the ignorant. We have all
known such—men and women in

whose hearts the love of God had been shed abroad, and whose lives through its influence had grown tender, unselfish, sympathetic— " living epistles of Christ known and read of all men. "

If I were asked, Why I believe in Jesus Christ? I should reply, Chiefly because of the characters He fashions. The Christ of the first century is commended to me by the lives of those in whose hearts He has been formed. I believe in the Word made flesh, very largely, through those who have become His Epistles—some of these are made known to me in history or biography ; others I have looked upon with my own eyes. Voltaire, after an interview with Fénélon, is reported to have said that what he saw in him was a greater proof of the truth of Christianity than all the books he had ever read in its defence. A youth once said that he could answer every argument for the

Christian faith but the saintly
life of his own mother. Surely
that in itself is the supreme
argument; for, if Christ came to
make saints, and if those saints
are made, He has verified His own
claims!

Of these men of the ancient
world, of whom we have been
thinking, it has been well said,
"There was no centre round
which they moved, no divine life
by which they were impelled; they
seemed to vanish and flee in un-
certain succession of light. But
Christianity, on the other hand,
glowed with a steady and unwav-
ering brightness. It not only
swayed the hearts of individuals,
by stirring them to their utmost
depths, but it moulded the laws of
nations, and regenerated the whole
condition of society. It gave to
mankind a fresh sanction in the
word of Christ, a powerful motive
in His love, an all-sufficient comfort in the life of immortality

made sure by His resurrection and
ascension."*

If you want a proof nearer, I
will suggest one to you. In this
land of ours all men are more or
less touched with the influence of
Christianity; but still there are
those who consciously and willingly
yield to its claims, and those who
do not. Compare these two classes;
get at their inner spirit; and then
ask yourselves: In which is conscience .keener, sympathy deeper,
love more dominant, hope brighter?
In which are efforts for the good
of others most earnest and sus-
tained? To ask is to answer
the question. You know that the
spirit of Christ makes for righteousness, sympathy, love, hope,
service for others. If it be so,
since these are all tokens of life—
the highest life—you have ample
proof that it is the Divine way for
men.

Thirdly, the expressions of this life.

* Cf. Farrar's "Seekers after God."

On this I need not linger. If the
life quickened by Christ be such
as I have described, the expressions
of it must be of a like nature.
"As a man thinketh in his heart
so is he," both in nature and its
expressions. The author of that
great book, "Ecce Homo," speaks
of the "enthusiasm of humanity"
as the characteristic expression of
Christianity. That is abundantly
ratified by the history of the
world. One fact is sufficient proof
of this. In all ages men have
suffered from sickness, accident,
bereavement; but, till the entrance
of Jesus Christ to our world, no
provision was made for those who,
through poverty, could not provide for themselves when these
troubles came upon them. Every
hospital is the direct outcome of
the new spirit wakened by Jesus
Christ. Before He came you will
seek such institutions in vain, even
in the most enlightened lands. The
Pagan religions never reared a hos-

pital. The philosophers of Greece
and Rome, with all their knowledge,
never put their hands to such a
work. And to-day the hospitals
reared in India and China have
been reared, not by the priests of
their native faiths, but by men
from over the seas, touched by the
Christian spirit. That one fact is
sufficient witness to the new spirit
wakened by Jesus Christ; and
that one fact is but the outward
and visible sign of an entire
change in the relationship between
men.

The time would fail to tell of
the numberless agencies of a like
kind which have grown out of this
new spirit, which cares for man as
man. Before, he was cared for
only in relation to the State. If
he could serve the State, he was
valued; if he could not, he was
cast like rubbish to the void. That
is not the case to-day. Men, to-
day, are suffering from numberless
evils. The poor are in many

districts packed closer than cattle, with no room to move, with insufficient air to breathe, under conditions which make purity difficult, if not impossible. Children are compelled to learn in our Board schools without food enough to nourish their brains. For the aged poor there is only the dreary provision of the workhouse. Yes, but we *do* trouble ourselves about these things; we *do* seek remedies while, in the ancient world, the evils would have gone on unheeded and uncared for. That is a mighty difference, for out of this care the remedy for these evils will in time arise.*

* Sir William Muir, in a comparison between Christian and Mohammedan ethics, well says: "The 'social evil' and intemperance prevalent in Christian lands are the strongest weapons in the armoury of Islam. We point, and justly, to the higher morality and civilisation of those who do observe the precepts of the Gospel, to the stricter unity and virtue which cement the family, but in vain; while the example of our great cities, and too often of our repre-

What has been actually done through the spirit of Christ is great. Every hospital, every asylum, every refuge, every orphanage, every society for the relief of distress, is the outcome of this spirit.

Christ was first incarnate in His own body. Then He incarnates Himself in His disciples, and, then, their quickened feeling incarnates itself in these institutions. These are the visible proofs of the Christ in the nineteenth century.

And almost equally great is the changed 'feeling which reckons nothing human alien to us—which reaches beyond the bounds of our own to other countries—which

sentatives abroad, belies the argument. And yet the argument is sound; for, in proportion as Christianity exercises her legitimate influence, vice and intemperance will wane and vanish, and the higher morality pervade the whole body; while, in Islam, the deteriorating influence of polygamy, divorce, and concubinage have been stereotyped for all time."—"The Coran," p. 62.

makes our Patriotism develop into Cosmopolitanism, and which will slowly, but surely, convert the world into a kingdom of God.

All these things of which I have spoken show that we have not followed cunningly devised fables when we accepted Jesus Christ as Lord. He is engaged in a great world-work. In Him alone the hope of the future is to be found, and I ask you to range yourselves under His banner, and bear your part in aiding Him to accomplish His great purpose—"I am come that they might have life, and that they might have it more abundantly." My friend, Alfred Hayes, closes his poem, "The March of Man," a poem socialistic in its trend, with these remarkable words, which I commend to all who imagine that the world can be regenerated without Christ:—

A mighty change,
Enfolded in the troubled womb of time,
Shapeth itself in silence; foolish hopes

And fond alarms disquiet faithless
    breasts;
Love waits the birth unfaltering.—The
    wise world
Hath not forgot how in a simple room
A Jewish craftsman with his fisher-
    friends
Once ate their farewell supper; high
    priests hissed
Their spite; Rome curled a lip of sickly
    scorn;
But life was with the little brother-band,
And mankind's slow salvation.—Love
    can wait.

The Change as Seen in the Christian Outlook on the Problems of the World.

"Therefore let us draw back from the sensuous charm of that 'private relationship with God.' When we turn to God we are not to feel that we are cut off from all other men, but that we are entering into fellowship with them. We believe that we are to look for God's care for our individual lives, but we are to expect that He will care only for that in our lives which belongs to the moral brotherhood, and not for that which refuses to enter into fellowship and so is cut off from the eternal."
—WILLIBALD HERRMANN.

THE CHANGE AS SEEN IN THE CHRISTIAN OUTLOOK ON THE PROBLEMS OF THE WORLD.

"For we are members one of another."—
EPHESIANS IV. 25.

IN previous lectures I have endeavoured to present the proof of Christianity in what it has done in the world :—in the change wrought by Christ in His first scholars :—the apostles : in the change on a larger scale from Paganism to Christendom : in the Christian life and character. These are all great changes—changes which amply support Christ's claim to be a life-giver to men.

But no one of these, nor all of them together, exhaust the work which Christ came to accomplish. Very much remains to be done,

before the world corresponds to
the ideal of Jesus Christ; there is
more land yet to be possessed.
Intensively, as well as extensively,
Christ has yet much to do in the
world. His power is adequate to
the work, but it has been frus-
trated, or, at least, hindered, by
human causes. One of these causes
I have already hinted at—the
unwillingness of men to give Him
entrance to their hearts, or to permit
Him to influence their lives. This
is probably the greatest hindrance
of all. But there have been other
hindrances, which have not been
conscious oppositions, but have
arisen from misconceptions as to
the nature and method of His
work.

This will be clear from one great
fact written across the face of the
Church's history—that the progress
of Christianity in the early ages
was very rapid, but that gradually
it became very much slower. Of
the rapidity of its progress take an

illustration or two. Just before
the final persecution of the Christians by Diocletian, at the opening
of the third century, Eusebius says,
"Who could describe those vast
collections of men that flocked to
the religion of Christ, and those
multitudes crowding in from every
city, and the illustrious concourse
in the houses of worship?" In
that persecution we read of
a town in Phrygia, burned with
all its population, because its
inhabitants, including women and
children, those in high rank as
well as persons of humbler station,
confessed themselves Christians,
and would not recant. In Ar-
menia, two-thirds of the people
may be reckoned as professing
Christians. So widespread was
the Christian faith that, as
Eusebius says, "Maxentius, the
usurper of imperial power in Italy,
sought to ingratiate himself with
the Romans by pretending that he
was of the Christian faith. Maxi-

7

min, Emperor of the East, the most obstinate and cruel of the persecutors, gave as a reason for the severity of his persecutions, that the emperors had seen that almost all men were abandoning the worship of the gods, and attaching themselves to the party of the Christians." And Lucian, of Antioch, says, "That, prior to the last persecution, almost the greater part of the world, including whole cities, had yielded obedience to the truth." * And all this in spite of repeated and cruel persecutions.

What, then, retarded the progress of Christianity? There were many causes for this. Of these I will briefly speak, since they present warnings for our own time.

When the Christian faith started on its victorious career, the apostles and their first converts were full of a passionate love to Jesus Christ.

* *Cf.* "Neglected Factors in the Study of the Early Progress of Christianity." By Dr. James Orr.

All their thoughts gathered around Him. So close were they drawn to Him, that they were drawn even closer to one another. Because they felt that one was their Master, even Christ, they felt that they were all brethren. That feeling led to the communism of the Apostolic Church. None called the things that were his, his own ; all things were freely shared.

Let me say in passing that is a communism to which none can object. A communism enforced by law from without is both impossible and undesirable ; but a communism prompted solely by love within the heart to the brethren around, is a thing to be admired, not blamed.

I refer to this only to show how deep and keen was the love-spirit that inspired the earliest converts. And, as long as that love-spirit continued, the onward march of the faith was rapid and uninterrupted. But gradually that spirit

waned : the Christ, as the supreme
object of the heart's affections,
gave place to doctrines about Him.
As love waned, as the heart fell
into the background, the mind
wanted to analyse the object of its
faith. Gradually faith in a personal Christ gave place to acceptance of doctrine concerning Him.

The Gospel came into contact
with the Greek mind, which de-
lights in subtle distinction, in
abstract thought, in philosophical
speculation.

It has been truly said that "we
owe many of our doctrines to the
restless deductiveness of the Greek
mind. A Jew could not have con-
ceived them, nor the mind of
Western Europe disengaged and
set them up. It is possible that
some of the distinctions and refine-
ments, which received the sanction
of the Church, would have been
altogether unintelligible to the
original disciples of our Lord. If
Christianity had made no Greek

converts, and had never been steeped in the atmosphere of Greek philosophy; if it had addressed itself only to the Latin and Teutonic races, such doctrines might not have been elicited from the Christian Scripture."*

If you would realise this, compare the answer given by Philip to the Ethiopian when he asked to be baptized, with, say, the Nicene Creed. Philip said, "If thou believest with all thine heart thou mayest," to which the Ethiopian replied, "I believe that Jesus Christ is the Son of God." The Council of Nicæa would have recited its creed, with its minute distinctions concerning the Divine Being, as necessary to salvation. Thus, you see, the simple personal object of faith gave way to highly complex doctrine, and too often the doctrine hid the person. "Faith in the thing became faith

* Cf. "Our Prayer-Book. Conformity and Conscience." By W. Page Roberts.

in the report "—to use Browning's expressive phrase.

I do not object to doctrinal forms, but they are harmful, to the last degree, when put in the place of the real object of faith—Jesus Christ. And when men went forth preaching doctrine instead of Christ, the glow, the inspiration, departed, and the progress of Christianity grew ever slower.

Another spirit passed into Christianity when it touched the Roman mind. The Greek wanted to analyse it, to reduce it to a philosophical system; but the Roman wanted to make an institution of it, with its officers, its laws, its ritual. He wanted to organise it. Well, there is no objection to organisation—life always clothes itself with an organism—from the life of a mollusc to that of a man, life must be clothed upon. The mischief comes in when the organisation, instead of expressing

the life, confines it, represses it,
crushes it. The child's life ex-
presses itself in its ever-growing
body ; but, put that child into a
suit of closely-fitting armour, and
growth is impossible. Rome
organised the Christian life almost
to death ; made men think more
of the officers of the Church than
the Church itself ; more of its laws
than the spirit they should express. And we are suffering the
result to-day, so that certain
people will not recognise a Church
as Christian, though it may be full
of Christ's spirit, full of good
works, except it have what is
called "The Historic Episcopate"
—that is, unless it be governed by
bishops in what is considered the
true apostolical succession. Thus
in the Roman world organisation
repressed, instead of expressing,
the life.

Then, beyond this, as time went
on, the scope of Christian purpose
was narrowed. Christ came to

give life—life more abundantly.
And if we may judge by His own
work and that of the apostles, His
purpose was to minister to the
whole life of man. In Christ's
work on earth no part of man's
nature was left out of account.
He ministered to body, mind,
spirit. No disease ever fronted
Christ with which He did not
grapple; not merely in proof of
His mission, but out of His deep
compassion for men. Then, He
was ever teaching, ever arousing
men's minds by quickening words.
Then, He was ever meeting the
highest needs of the spirit by His
revelation of the Father. Christ
came to give life, and life runs
through every part of the complex
nature of man. It cannot be shut
in any little enclosure of his being.
But, gradually, men narrowed
down Christ's work to one part of
the being, which they called the
soul. And too often all the food
supplied to that was mere abstract

doctrine, which was regarded as essential to eternal life. Instead of the fresh flowers of the Gospel field, with all their fragrance and beauty, men were offered the dried and labelled specimens of the museum, from which the colour, the form, the fragrance had departed.

Then, beyond this, some of the characteristic features of the Gospel grew conspicuous by their absence. If there be one thing more characteristic than another of Christ's ministry, it is that He came to reveal the Father. That word Father is the dominant note in the melody of the Gospel. How sweet and beautiful it is! How all-inclusive, when rightly regarded, it is! Yes, but in the Greek thought the Fatherhood became too vague and far off to have any power. In the Roman's thought the Father disappeared, and the king on the throne, or the judge on the bench of heaven, took His place.

Has the Gospel ever had a fair chance when its characteristic message has been so seldom heard, or changed into one of an utterly different type?

Speaking of the gradual corruption of the Christian Church, the author of " Ecce Homo " says —" The bridal dress is worn out, and the orange flower is faded. First, the rottenness of dying superstitions, then barbaric manners, then intellectualism, preferring system and debate to brotherhood, strangling Christianity with theories — all these corruptions have, in the successive ages of its long life, infected the Church."

In spite of all this, it has done wonders; it has almost turned the world upside down. But if, through all ages, the real message of the Gospel had been spoken, and spoken with the only spirit appropriate to it—the spirit of love —by this time, the world would have been redeemed unto God.

But, thank God, we are now beginning to see Christ as the first converts to Christianity saw Him. There has been, of late, a return to the simplicity of Christ. This age of ours is becoming Christocentric—that is, Christ is becoming the centre of all our thought and all our inspiration. When the ancient king asked the philosopher what he could do for him, he replied, " Get out of the light! " And this age is beginning to say to the theologians, unless you can reveal Christ to us more clearly, get out of the light that we may see Him for ourselves.

I daresay some of you think it strange that it has taken all these centuries for men to get back to the reality of Jesus Christ, to that peerless life beneath the Syrian blue, that life, so short in ministry, but so marvellous in its after issues. Yes, it is strange; but is it not equally strange that it took many thousands of years for men to get at the truth of the world upon which they dwell? From the beginning it has been moving, but till quite recent times men thought it stationary. From the beginning the sun has been stationary, but men thought it moving. And, all the time, the earth moved under their feet and the sun stood still before their eyes. If men made such mistakes about things they could see, is it any wonder that they made like mistakes about a Christ who had passed out of their sight? For, after all, things unseen—things spiritual—are harder to reach than things material, — things seen. Men are less willing to seek the spiritual than the material; and, for an obvious reason,—they can seek the material without any change of course or spirit, but they cannot rightly seek the spiritual without changes of life and action, and these they are not willing to make.

But this age of ours is beginning

to see that life depends upon the spiritual far more than on the material. As Mr. Kidd reminds us, our age has been reinforced with a flood of altruistic energy, so that it is beginning to feel that the truest and happiest course is to look, not on our own things, but also on the things of others. This is a return to Christ, to His teaching, to His spirit. And out of this great results may be expected.

There is plenty of work for this new spirit to do. In the first age of the Church how much it accomplished! It was this spirit, which lies at the very heart of Christianity, that more than anything else turned that ancient world upside down. The first Christians were few, feeble, poor, unlettered, but this spirit in them made them "mighty through God to the pulling down of strongholds."

In its retrospect of the year 1898 *The Daily Telegraph* spoke of " The

almost measureless strength which
England commands." Oh, what
wonders might be accomplished, if
that almost measureless strength
were to be touched with the spirit
of Jesus Christ! Were it thus,
the early triumphs of the Church
would be thrown into the shade.

And that I submit to you is the
grand object for which we should
strive—not to confine our care to
the particular Church to which we
belong, not even to the whole
Church of Christ, but to bring in
the Kingdom of God upon earth.
That is the prayer we utter every
Sunday, and, it may be, every day,
"Thy kingdom come." That
prayer is Christ's. It is in harmony with all His teaching and
all His work. He scarcely ever
spoke of the Church—the word
Church is only found twice in the
gospels—but He was ever speaking
of the Kingdom of God, or, what
is the same thing, the Kingdom of
Heaven. And the Kingdom is

larger than the Church—the Church is but the means; the Kingdom is the end it should seek.

And a Kingdom of God on earth will not be set up till every man has his place as a citizen therein. And citizenship means both rights and duties; rights—which surely include space to live, means of living, access to what belongs to the kingdom; duties—to serve and further the varied interests of the kingdom.

How far we are at present from these conditions! Multitudes have not space to live. In our great cities the struggle for places of abode has reached an awful crisis. It is heartrending to read the reports of efforts to get a single room, into which a whole family is crowded, to pay for which a large portion of the breadwinner's earnings has to be spent—a rent out of all proportion to the accommodation secured, or the state of the apartments.

I have felt for years that, in our great cities, it is the exorbitant rents that have to be paid which cripple the poor in their struggle for existence. Some years ago I was in the East End of London, and, in conjunction with a doctor-friend, I made a calculation on this matter, and I found that the poor who dwell in single rooms pay far more than double the price for them which the inhabitants in the larger houses in the same district do for theirs. My friend lived in a house of £40 a year; that house let to the poor, in apartments, would have brought in more than £100 a year.

This is not the place to go into the reasons for this, but let Christian people remember that religion has no chance with people herded together like cattle. Why, even morality is difficult, if not impossible.

Then think of the fierce struggle for existence that goes on, the result of ever keener competition, leading to sweating and other enormities, every moment of the day, sometimes far into the night, employed to complete the work necessary to keep off starvation. Is it possible to believe that God ever meant His children to lead lives of never-ceasing work, with no leisure for rest or recreation? Why, even horses are better off, for their owners see that they are not overworked to the detriment of their strength; but, then, horses are valuable, and human lives are often not so regarded.

Think, too, of the lot of little children under such conditions, deprived, as infants, of proper and needed maternal care—their mothers so occupied with work, that no time for nurture of their children is left; and then, a little later, sent to school with sickly bodies, unfit to bear the strain of lessons, with too little food to invigorate their brains; taken away

at the very earliest moment, to
help their parents in the struggle
for existence; and before very
long forced by the straitness of
the home, or the cruelty of their
parents, to start life for themselves;
led thus into improvident marriages, which only add to the
general sum of misery. The heart
aches at it all. Sometimes the
very pleasure of the sunlight and
the beauty of nature are over-
shadowed to me by the thought
of the numbers who do not share
in these provisions of the great
Father.

Now, I can barely touch the
causes of this state of things; they
are manifold. Some of them are
due to faults of the people themselves—drinking, thriftlessness, im-
providence, too early marriages;
but some of them are due to
wrongs in the social order. And
both causes need remedies.

For the faults of the people I
know of no remedy but loving and

personal ministry : the arousing of
the better nature by the gospel of
the grace of God, through the
words and influence of His followers. But this is far more difficult to be applied than formerly,
since most of those who could
render such services now live so
far away from the degraded neigh-
bourhoods. Formerly the rich and
the poor, employers and employed,
dwelt near to one another ; now
they live miles apart—the employed in the slums, the employers
in the suburbs. The distance
between them makes it far harder
to render the kindly help which
would otherwise be forthcoming.
University settlements may do
something, but I fear they do
not reach the lowest; their work
is probably with the better class of
artizan. But *there* is the work to
be done, and it ought to lie like a
heavy weight on our Christian
conscience until it is done. I often
feel that some of the agencies

in operation in the suburbs ought
to be transferred to degraded districts, where are multitudes who
need them far more. There, in the
great city, are the workers without
whom those in the suburbs could
not live. Surely some efforts should
be put forth for their good. Let
the Church think of it, and Christian ingenuity will gradually devise
a means of grappling with the
difficult problem.

I rejoice to know that many
employers *do* interest themselves
in the lives of those in their service. Ah! that is good. Much
may be done in that way; but,
alas! alas! to many employers
those who do their work are
only "hands." How I hate that
word! What a revelation it is of
inner feeling! And such toilers
are cast, it seems to me, on the
help of those who bear Christ's
name and are thereby pledged to
the relief of the needy.

But then, as I have said, there

are causes of poverty not due to
the individual, but to the present
social order. That order is the
result of unjust laws made in the
past, made when the Government
was in the hands of the wealthy,
laws chiefly made for their own
protection. What Government
has done, in this respect, can only
be undone by the same authority.
The kingdom of God will not be
brought in, as some think, by
legislation, but just laws must be
passed to provide the conditions
necessary to the coming of the
kingdom.

Sir John Seeley has well said,
"Christ commanded His first
followers to heal the sick and give
alms, but He commands the Christians of this age, if we may use
the expression, to investigate the
causes of all physical evil, to master
the science of health, to consider
the question of education with a
view to health, the question of
labour with a view to health, the

question of trade with a view to
health ; and while all these inves-
tigations are made, with free ex-
pense of energy and time and
means, to work out the re-arrange-
ment of life in accordance with the
results they give."*

Now, what is the true relation
of the Church to such matters ?
Some there are who would have
the Church deal with political
questions; that is the idea on
which what are called Labour
Churches are founded. The gospel
preached in them is chiefly a
political one. Some there are who
would have the pulpit deal with
such questions, and the Church
pass political resolutions. That
would only introduce a new division
among the churches into Conser-
vative and Liberal. I shall always
claim the right to exercise my
judgment as a citizen on matters
political, and to vote according to
my conscience, but I shall never

* "Ecce Homo," p. 202.

make the pulpit the vantage ground for political discourse. Jesus Christ never touched politics. He refused to interfere either in matters political or legal. When the request was made, "Master, bid my brother divide the inheritance with me," He replied, "Man, who made Me a judge or a divider over you?" When they showed Him a Roman coin, and asked whose image and superscription is this? He replied, "Render to Cæsar the things that are Cæsar's, and to God the things that are God's." He cried, "My kingdom is not of this world, else would My servants fight, but now is My kingdom not from hence." When they would come and take Him by force to make Him a king, who, of course, could make laws, He departed to a mountain alone. And the Apostles acted along the same lines. They went first to the Roman Empire, and found fronting them everywhere the monstrous iniquity of slavery. Did they agitate against it? Did they preach against it? No. But they created such an atmosphere of brotherhood that before it slavery gradually disappeared.

There are those who would bring in communism by State enactments, and they sometimes point to the community of goods of the Early Church. But that came about not by outward enactment, but inward inspiration. The fervour of love moved the heart, which soon opened the hand. The vast changes wrought in early times by Christianity were wrought, not by political but, by spiritual forces.

And this is the example for the Church of to-day. Where the social order needs altering, it is not for her to enter upon a political campaign, but so to kindle the sense of God's fatherhood, and of man's brotherhood, that such an atmosphere will be created that righteous laws will be inevitable. This is the task of the Church in

relation to the improvement of the
social order. In it every Christian,
however humble, should have a
part. Some influence belongs to
each one of us. This should be used,
not merely to increase the extent
or wealth of our empire, but to give
each member of it his just place at
the great table of God.

For, remember, the miseries of
the world do not arise out of insufficient Divine provision, but out
of unjust human distribution. God
has made ample provision, but it is
unfairly divided. Not many years
ago, the fear prevailed that the
food of the world would be insufficient for its ever-growing population. That fear has passed. Indeed, the trouble now is that food
is so plentiful that it does not pay
the human producers. God is not
at fault, but men are.

And the great object before the
Church should be, on the one
hand, to make the poor more
thrifty, sober, industrious, and, on

the other hand, so to improve the
social order that, for all who will
work, there may be sufficient return
to provide food, home, the means
of recreation and improvement—in
a word, to give to every creature of
God his proper share in the great
Father's provision.

" As the early Christians learnt
that it was not enough to do no
harm, and that they were bound to
give meat to the hungry and clothing to the naked, we have learnt
that a still further obligation lies
upon us, to prevent, if possible, the
pains of hunger and nakedness
from being ever felt." *

And the Gospel, rightly under-
stood and applied, will accomplish
this ; for, on the one hand, it will so
uplift the individual that he will become active, thrifty, foreseeing; and
it will make the social order so just,
so considerate, so careful of the
rights of all, that not a few, but
all, will have a fair opportunity of

* " Ecce Homo," p. 107.

becoming what God would have them be, strong in body, enlightened in mind, pure in spirit—in a word, the sons of God without offence.

I cannot conclude these lectures without reference to a fact by which Christianity is differentiated from all other religions—that it believes it will one day be the one faith for the world. No other religion has ever had so grand a confidence. In this respect Judaism, the faith out of which Christianity sprang, falls infinitely short of its greater child. Judaism, save in the case of certain lofty spirits, such as the greater prophets, rather gloried in its exclusiveness, and sought to perpetuate it. Other faiths, like Mohammedanism and Buddhism, have been to some extent missionary, but always within certain narrow limits. Mohammedanism never attempted to force her way farther West than Spain, whilst Buddhism has never sought to pass beyond the nations of the East.

But Christianity has dreams of a world-wide empire—dreams which are fast passing into the realm of reality.

Already her sacred message has been translated into every, or nearly every, language under heaven—in many cases into languages which had to be reduced to writing before the work of translation could be commenced. The late Isaac Taylor regarded this as the special work of our age—as a seed-sowing, whose plentiful harvest would appear later in the world's history.

In every land the Christian missionary is at work, and everywhere with more or less success.

The very fact that the Gospel can be made intelligible to the peoples of the East and the West, the North and the South, is one of supreme significance, for it proves that its message appeals, not to the elements in which men differ,

but to those in which they agree—
not to the superficial, but the basal
elements of human nature.

It is in harmony with this idea
that Jesus Christ gave the world,
not detailed rules for life, which
must differ with the various ages
and lands, but great principles,
which can adapt themselves to the
changed conditions wrought by
the lapse of time, and the differ-
ing natures of men in various
lands.

Before its message, the other
faiths of the world are beginning
to fade. The nearest exception to
this is Mohammedanism, and that,
it may be, because it has borrowed
so largely from Judaism — the
parent stock of Christianity. Over
every other faith is slowly creep-
ing the conviction that they
must pale their ineffectual fires
before the greater light of Him,
in whom is neither Greek
nor Jew, Barbarian, Scythian,
bond nor free, but who is in the

deepest sense the "Desire of all
the nations," at whose feet they
all, at last, shall gather, and find
rest unto their souls.

And the very fact that Christianity thus fronts the world, in
spite of the fears of faithless
hearts, in spite of the sneers of
the critics, is in itself no mean
argument for its truth.

"The Sermon on the Mount is a
cosmopolitan sermon; it speaks to
no age, for it addresses every age
and every nation. It appeals to
no national characteristics, for it
deals with those qualities which
lie beneath all nationality, and
which tend, not so much to distinguish man from man, as to
distinguish man from all other
creatures of creation."*

Call it a dream if you will, but
it is, at least, a dream such as no
other faith has ever had, and the
very dream, if dream it be, is the

* Matheson's "Growth of the Spirit of
Christianity," vol. I., p. 44.

outgrowth of a sublime confidence on the part of believers that their Master is no mere national leader, but the Saviour of the World.

But it is a dream which is growing to incarnation in fact; slowly, but surely, Jesus Christ is advancing to the fulfilment of His grand declaration: "I, if I be lifted up from the earth, will draw all men unto Me."

"Wheresoever Christianity has breathed it has accelerated the movement of humanity. It has quickened the pulses of life: it has stimulated the incentives to thought:—it has turned the passions into peace:—it has warmed the heart into brotherhood: it has fanned the imagination into genius: it has freshened the soul into purity. The progress of Christian Europe has been the progress of mind over matter. It has been the progress of intellect over force, of political right over arbitrary power, of human liberty over the chains of slavery, of moral law over social corruption, of order over anarchy, of enlightenment over ignorance, of life over death."*

"If this be so, has Christ failed, or can Christianity die?"

* Dr. G. Matheson's "Growth of the Spirit of Christianity." Vol. II., p. 394.

Those who desire to gain fuller information on the argument presented in these lectures should consult the following works :

THE GENTILE AND JEW IN THE COURTS OF THE TEMPLE OF CHRIST. By Dr. Döllinger. (A book unfortunately out of print.)

GESTA CHRISTI. By C. Loring Brace.

THE DIVINE ORIGIN OF CHRISTIANITY. By Dr. R. S. Storrs.

SEEKERS AFTER GOD. By Dean Farrar.

NEGLECTED FACTORS IN THE STUDY OF THE EARLY PROGRESS OF CHRISTIANITY. By Dr. James Orr.

ECCE HOMO. By Sir John Seeley.

A MANUAL OF CHRISTIAN EVIDENCES. By the Rev. C. A. Row, M.A.

THE GROWTH OF THE SPIRIT OF CHRISTIANITY. By the Rev. George Matheson, D.D.

Certain works of fiction will be found helpful, such as :—

QUO VADIS. By Henryk Sienkiewicz.

DARKNESS AND DAWN. By Dean Farrar.

9

BY THE SAME AUTHOR.

THE TREASURY OF AMERICAN SACRED SONG. (10s. 6d.)

Henry Frowde,
Oxford University Press Warehouse.

WORSHIP SONG. A Hymnal.
(From 1s. to 8s.)

Elliot Stock.

THE POETS' BIBLE. 2 Vols.
(3s. 6d. each.)

Ward, Lock and Co.

THE SILENT VOICE, and Other Discourses. (3s. 6d.)

Isbister and Co., Limited.

THE HYMN LOVER. (5s.)

Curwen and Sons.

THE AMBITIONS OF ST. PAUL.
(1s. 6d.)

Alexander and Shepheard.

QUAKER WORTHIES. (2s. 6d. & 1s. 6d.)

Headley Brothers.

IS THERE A FUTURE LIFE?
(3s. 6d.)

Elliot Stock.

Any of the above books may be obtained of the Publishers of this Volume,

JAMES CLARKE & CO., 13, FLEET STREET.

LONDON:
W. SPEAIGHT AND SONS, PRINTERS,
FETTER LANE.